A SIENA BOOK

Siena is an imprint of Parragon Books
Published by Parragon Book Service Ltd,
Units 13-17, Avonbridge Trading Estate, Atlantic Road,
Avonmouth, Bristol BS11 9QD

Produced by The Templar Company plc,
Pippbrook Mill, London Road, Dorking, Surrey RH4 1JE

Edited by Robert Snedden
Designed by Mark Summersby

Printed and bound in Great Britain

ISBN 0-75250-833-4

I like to read

Dotty Dog's Seaside Adventure

Written by Julia Stanton
Illustrated by Kate Sheppard

SIENA

Dotty Dog's Seaside Adventure

It is summer. Bill Bear, Rollo Rabbit and Dotty Dog are going to the seaside. Rollo Rabbit will drive the car.

What will they take with them? Rollo Rabbit wants to take his blue bucket and his red spade. Bill Bear wants to take his green flying disc and pink ball.

Dotty Dog wants to take her striped beach towel, her sunglasses, and her yellow hat. She also wants to take her beach umbrella, her radio, and her toy dinosaur. But she can't take them all!

Rollo Rabbit drives out of the town and down the hill. They go past the woods and through the tunnel. Bill Bear sits on the front seat beside Rollo. Dotty Dog sits on the back seat.

When they arrive at the seaside, the sun is shining. Bill Bear and Rollo Rabbit make a sandcastle. Dotty Dog sunbathes.

It is very hot. Bill Bear and
Rollo Rabbit want to cool
down. They go for a swim.
They play in the waves.
Dotty Dog falls asleep.

Dotty Dog has a dream. She is the captain of a pirate ship. Bill Bear and Rollo Rabbit are pirates. She is looking for the Bearded Pirate.

There is a great battle.
Bill Bear and Rollo Rabbit
jump into the water. Dotty
Dog feels someone pulling
her tail!

Dotty Dog wakes up. The crab runs away. Dotty Dog is pleased that it was only a dream. It is time to leave the seaside. The friends go home for tea.

What are the friends doing?

swimming

driving

sunbathing

sleeping

jumping

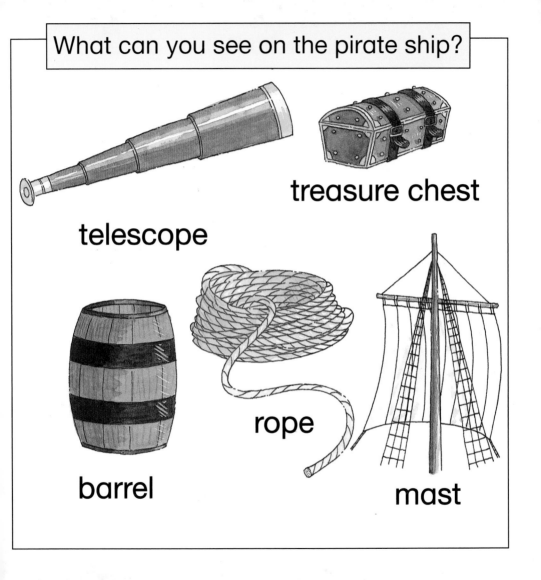

What can you see on the pirate ship?

telescope

treasure chest

barrel

rope

mast

past the woods

through the tunnel

under the sea

out of the town

Who do these things belong to?

yellow hat

sunglasses

green flying disc

toy dinosaur

red spade